MOVING TO TOWN

MOVING TO TOWN

Mattie Lou O'Kelley

Little, Brown and Company
Boston   Toronto   London

Books by Mattie Lou O'Kelley

Circus!

From the Hills of Georgia
An Autobiography in Paintings

A Winter Place
by Ruth Radin

Mattie Lou O'Kelley would like to thank Michael McKelvey,
who photographed her paintings for this book.

First Edition

Library of Congress Cataloging-in-Publication Data

O'Kelley, Mattie Lou.
    Moving to town / written and illustrated by Mattie Lou O'Kelley.
    — 1st ed.
       p.   cm.
    Summary: A rural family moves from their old farm to a house in the big city.
    ISBN 0-316-63805-6
    [1. Moving, Household — Fiction.   2. City and town life — Fiction.]
I. Title.
PZ7.04145Mo   1991
[E] — dc20   90-40328

Joy Street Books are published by Little, Brown and Company (Inc.)

10 9 8 7 6 5 4 3 2 1

WOR

Published simultaneously in Canada
by Little, Brown & Company (Canada) Limited

Printed in the United States of America

For T. Marshall Hahn, Jr.,
a great fellow and a Southern gentleman

We're moving! When spring came, at last Papa said we could move to town. No more crops to harvest! Mama said, "Pile everything in the hall. We'll load the wagon from the front porch." Johnnie and I were so excited we ran and jumped right in the middle of the big fat mattresses.

Off at last! Three wagons full. Lillie squeezed in next to Gert and Ruth while Tom and Ben helped Willie finish loading. Papa called our dogs, Buck and Scott, and they ran up alongside us. Spring was in the air and Mama said, "That plowed field sure smells good." "The city will be different," Papa said. I couldn't wait to find out what it would be like.

I could see everything from my seat way up high on top of the big bed in the first wagon. We hadn't gone far when suddenly Papa cried, "Woah! What's happened here?" The bridge was down. "Now we won't be able to get to the city," Johnnie whispered to me. "Your Pa will handle this," Mama said. We had to go the long way around.

We slowly started up the hill on the new mountain road. Buck and Scott ran ahead. It was so steep I thought our horses would never make it. Johnnie was getting cranky. "When are we going to get to the city?" he kept asking. Of course, I was fizzing to get there too, but I tried to be patient. "Shhh," said Mama, "you children keep quiet. Can't you see your Pa is trying not to fall off this mountain?"

When it got dark we made camp. Once the cows and the mules were fed, we got to have our fried chicken and biscuits. "Now everybody jump in bed," Papa ordered. Johnnie said, "But I want to play in the branch." "Me too!" I said real big, "I want to play in the branch too!" It was so quiet and dark, we could see the stars clear as anything.

Papa got us up with the sun and we were on our way. We passed lots of farms below us, and then we started going down, down, down until suddenly Johnnie jumped straight up, quick as lightning. "It's the city! The city!" he yelled. "I can't believe we're really here," Mama said real quiet. "How will we ever find our house?" I just couldn't believe my two eyes. I'd never seen so many big buildings!

"There it is — our house!" Papa said big and loud. I was so busy looking every which way I missed it. "Where? Where?" Papa pointed to a little white house on the hill. "The man said we'd see it when we came to the S road. He said it used to be the town watchman's house." Johnnie jumped up and down. "I can't wait," he said. "Buck and Scott can't wait either," I said. "Look, they're almost there already."

Lillie took us all around town the very next day. She lined us up like marbles and pointed out everything from the streetcars to the policeman. "Now I'm going off to look for a job," she said. "Don't you little kids get lost. If you need help, just ask that man in the blue uniform." "Ben and I are going to see it all," Tom said. Ben giggled. "You bet."

Johnnie and I might be little, but we had Buck and Scott with us. They found this place with all kinds of funny-looking animals fenced in. The policeman there was nice as pie. "Welcome to the zoo," he said. "You kids hold on to your dogs and just follow the crowds." We saw polar bears, flamingos, giraffes, and even big lions and elephants — just like we learned about in school!

On the way home we passed the biggest house I'd ever seen. The man on the bench said it was a hospital — a place for sick people. "When we get sick we stay in our *own* bed," Johnnie said. "Mama gives us castor oil." "And hot coffee with milk in it," I said, "and buttered biscuits with homemade blackberry jam." I sure hoped I wouldn't get sick while we were in the city!

Lillie got a job in a big restaurant. One night she took us all there for dinner. She called it "eating out." I'd never "eaten out" before and I didn't know what to do! Lillie told us to just look at the menu and order anything we wanted. I couldn't decide — it all looked so good. But when it finally came it wasn't nearly as good as Mama's. I gave Buck and Scott a taste when nobody was looking.

One day we went shopping. I had never heard such a racket! "They even have *ice cream*," I said. "I see some watermelons," Johnnie yelled. "Let's get one!" "But we don't have any money," I said. "You have to have money to get watermelons in the city." "I'd rather get it off the vine myself, anyway," Johnnie said. "I need to thump it first. That way I know if it's really ripe."

Downtown it was real crowded. One day we heard lots of shouting and went up on the roof to see what all the commotion was about. "I see, I see — it's a runaway horse!" I said. But Johnnie wasn't interested. "Buck is scared being up this high," Johnnie said. "Let's go back down."

THE RAINBOW TRAIN

Summer was almost over. One day, after a rain, we walked just outside the city to see the rainbow. "I see a train in that rainbow," Johnnie said. "You're telling stories," I said. "I don't see a thing." What I did see were people in the hills around us picking cotton. It made me miss the farm.

SCHOOL HOUSE

Before we knew it, it was the first day of school. "What a place!" I said. "It's so big," Johnnie said. "I'll get lost in that great big building." "I'll help you," I said, "and Buck and Scott will be right outside waiting for us at the end of the day."

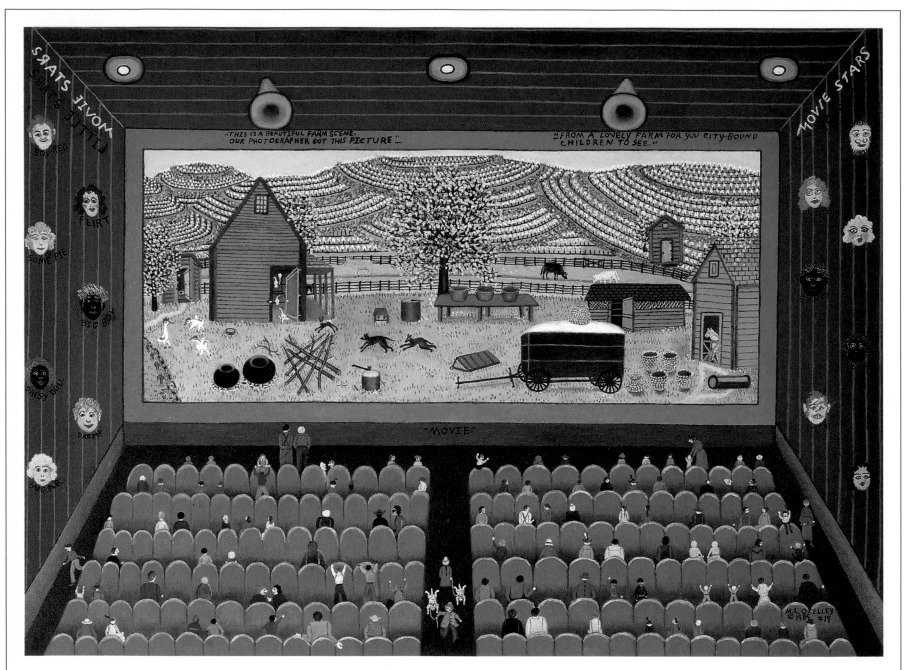

One Saturday afternoon we went to our first movie. It was all about growing up on a farm. When we saw the animals, Johnnie and I wished we could see our own cows and chickens again. We liked the movie so much, we stayed to see it again. Then Johnnie jumped up and said, "We're late for dinner — hurry up!" I didn't want to leave.

TURREY AND ALL

I couldn't believe it was already Thanksgiving. Lillie was home from work, and the whole house smelled good. Papa got a turkey from the butcher in town, and Mama made apple and pecan pie and pumpkin cake. Johnnie and I just couldn't wait for dinner. Mama said cold weather was on the way. "A real buster," she said. "You'll have to wear your thick coats when you go out."

It was cold, all right. Johnnie and I almost got our tails blown off! Snow just fell out of the sky. Johnnie said he wished a real big storm would come. "Me too," I said, "no school! If we were back on the farm we could go sledding."

In early December we hurried down to Main Street to watch the big Christmas parade. All at once Santa Claus was right before our eyes. "Look!" I could hardly believe it. Johnnie let out a shout. "He won't know where our new house is! Let's run and tell him!" "Don't worry," I said, "he'll know."

Hurray! Papa told us we're going to move back to the country in time for Christmas! We hurried home to help pack .

Mama and Papa went ahead in the wagon. We followed right behind in the buggy with Lillie. It was so cold Buck and Scott got to ride up front with us. When we drove through the village Mary and Bobbie ran out to wave at us.

As we got closer Johnnie said, "I know where we are — around this curve, over the river, up the hill, and we're home!"

"What a surprise!" Our neighbors were already there to help us fix the place up. Mr. Woods lit a fire, and everyone pitched in. Buck and Scott rolled by the fire to get warm. We did too.

Christmas Day! What a day! Such a crowd! Lillie played the organ just like always. Papa said, "I like listening to her music even better than eating!" I got a big doll. Johnnie got a red wagon. Candy! Oranges! Good bananas! Johnnie and I just stood by the doorway with our mouths hanging open. It sure was good to be home.

About the Author

Mattie Lou O'Kelley was born in 1908 and grew up with her seven brothers and sisters and hardworking parents on a 129-acre hill farm in Maysville, Georgia. She labored on that family farm for close to half her life, picking cotton and making quilts, watering livestock and canning vegetables. It wasn't until the age of forty-seven that she first started to paint as a hobby, using a set of paints she ordered from the Sears and Roebuck catalog. Drawing on childhood memories and her rich imagination, she created finely detailed paintings notable for their variety of design and texture. When she was almost sixty years old and turned her full attention to painting, the American folk art world took notice.

In 1976 she was selected as a recipient of the Governor's Award in the Arts for the state of Georgia. Her work is now featured in the permanent collections of several museums here and abroad and has been published in three children's books and one adult book. Many of her paintings, including those she created especially for this book, document the small-town life of agrarian Georgia in the early 1900s.

Now eighty-three years old, Ms. O'Kelley paints all day in her home outside Atlanta, not far from the hill farm where she grew up. Painted with daring, beautiful colors she mixes herself and alive with her own special vision, her canvases glow with the richness and intricacy of fine needlework. Best of all, they tell wonderful stories. In *Moving to Town* her love of family and homestead and the wonder of experiencing life in the city for the first time are intimately revealed in her own lively, unique voice and in painting after heartfelt painting.